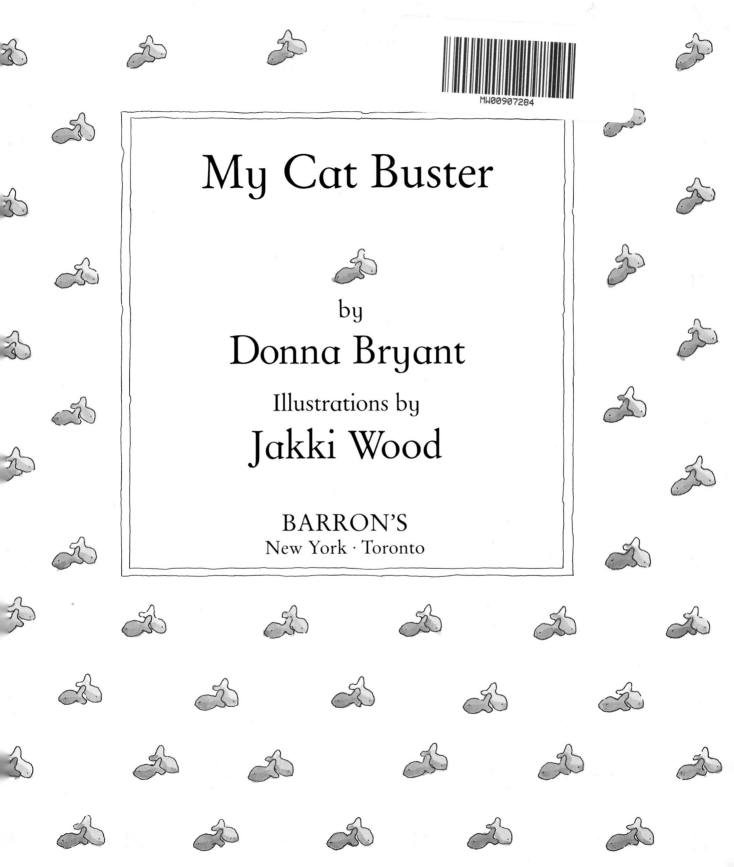

My Cat Buster

by

Donna Bryant

Illustrations by

Jakki Wood

BARRON'S
New York · Toronto

Buster wakes me every morning,

and pounces when I move my toes.

He likes some kinds of cat food,

and he loves cream.

He is very good at balancing

and swinging.

He loves things that fly,

and things that creep.

Buster likes to play...

and hide.

He is very good at washing...

just like me!

He will sleep anywhere.

His favorite place is on my clothes.

Sometimes Buster likes to be alone,

but he comes to me when I'm sad.

When I stroke him gently he purrs.

I love Buster. He's my friend.

First edition for the United States, Canada, and the Philippines
published 1991 by Barron's Educational Series, Inc.

Text © Copyright 1991 by Donna Bryant
Illustrations © Copyright 1991 by Jakki Wood

My Cat Buster was conceived, edited, and produced by
Frances Lincoln Ltd, Apollo Works, 5 Charlton Kings Road,
London NW5 2SB

All inquiries should be addressed to:
Barron's Educational Series, Inc.
250 Wireless Boulevard
Hauppauge, New York 11788

International Standard Book No. 0-8120-6211-6
Library of Congress Catalog Card No. 90-47925

Library of Congress Cataloging-in-Publication Data
Bryant, Donna.
My cat Buster / by Donna Bryant : Illustrations by Jakki Wood.
p. cm.
Summary: A child describes his favorite pet.
ISBN 0-8120-6211-6
[1. Cat–Fiction.] I. Wood, Jakki, ill. II. Title.
PZ7.B837Mv 1991
(E)–dc20   90-47925
                                                                   CIP
                                                                    AC

PRINTED IN HONG KONG
1234 0987654321